CECILY PARSLEY'S
NURSERY RHYMES

CECILY PARSLEY'S
NURSERY RHYMES

BY

BEATRIX POTTER

Author of
"The Tale of Peter Rabbit," etc.

FREDERICK WARNE

*The reproductions in this book have been made using
the most modern electronic scanning methods from entirely
new transparencies of Beatrix Potter's original watercolours.
They enable Beatrix Potter's skill as an artist to be appreciated
as never before, not even during her own lifetime.*

The originals of the illustrations on pages 17 and 30 are unavailable,
so a first edition has been photographed to reproduce these pictures.

FREDERICK WARNE

Penguin Books Ltd, Harmondsworth, Middlesex, England
Viking Penguin Inc., 40 West 23rd Street, New York, New York 10010, U.S.A
Penguin Books Australia Ltd, Ringwood, Victoria, Australia
Penguin Books Canada Limited, 2801 John Street, Markham, Ontario, Canada L3I
Penguin Books (N.Z.) Ltd, 182–190 Wairau Road, Auckland 10, New Zealand

Colour reproduction by
East Anglian Engraving Company Ltd, Norwich
Printed and bound in Great Britain by
William Clowes Limited, Beccles and London

1186

FOR
LITTLE PETER IN NEW ZEALAND

CECILY PARSLEY lived in
a pen,
And brewed good ale for
gentlemen;

GENTLEMEN came every
day,
Till Cecily Parsley ran away.

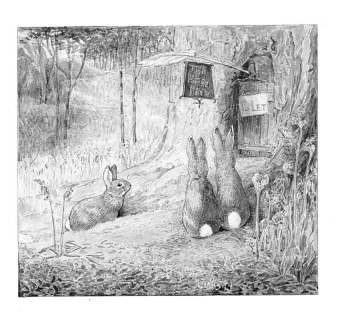

GOOSEY, goosey, gander,
    Whither will you wander?
Upstairs and downstairs,
    And in my lady's cham-
      ber!

THIS pig went to market ;
This pig stayed at home ;

THIS pig had a bit of meat ;

AND this pig had none ;

THIS little pig cried
    Wee ! wee ! wee !
I can't find my way home.

PUSSY-CAT sits by the
fire ;
How should she be fair ?
In walks the little dog,
Says "Pussy! are you there?"

"HOW do you do, Mistress
Pussy?
Mistress Pussy, how do
you do?"
"I thank you kindly, little dog,
I fare as well as you!"

THREE blind mice, three
　　blind mice,
　　See how they run !
They all run after the farmer's
　　wife,
And she cut off their tails with
　　a carving knife,
Did ever you see such a thing
　　in your life
　　As three blind mice !

BOW, wow, wow !
    Whose dog art thou ?
" I'm little Tom Tinker's dog,
    Bow, wow, wow ! ''

WE have a little garden,
    A garden of our own,
And every day we water there
    The seeds that we have
    sown.

WE love our little garden,
   And tend it with such care,
You will not find a faded leaf
   Or blighted blossom there.

NINNY NANNY NETTI-
   COAT,
In a white petticoat,
   With a red nose,—
The longer she stands,
   The shorter she grows.

The "PETER RABBIT" BOOKS
by BEATRIX POTTER

PETER RABBIT · SQUIRREL NUTKIN
TAILOR OF GLOUCESTER · BENJAMIN BUNNY
TWO BAD MICE · MRS. TIGGY–WINKLE
MR. JEREMY FISHER · TOM KITTEN
JEMIMA PUDDLE-DUCK · THE FLOPSY BUNNIES
MRS. TITTLEMOUSE · TIMMY TIPTOES
JOHNNY TOWN-MOUSE · MR. TOD
PIGLING BLAND · SAMUEL WHISKERS
THE PIE & THE PATTY-PAN · GINGER & PICKLES
LITTLE PIG ROBINSON

A FIERCE BAD RABBIT   MISS MOPPET
APPLEY DAPPLY'S   CECILY PARSLEY'S
NURSERY RHYMES   NURSERY RHYMES
PETER RABBIT'S   TOM KITTEN'S
PAINTING BOOK   PAINTING BOOK